AT THE END OF THE DAY I BURST INTO FLAMES

NICHOLAS DAY

Also by **Nicholas Day**

Novels

GRIND YOUR BONES TO DUST

Novellas

OCTOBER ANIMALS

NECROSAURUS REX

Short Story Collections

NOBODY GETS HURT AND OTHER LIES

NOW THAT WE'RE ALONE

INTRODUCTION

By Sara Tantlinger

Do you have a fire inside of you?

Surely, there is something that burns within your depths, perhaps in the pit of your stomach or with flames beneath your heart. I think we all have a bit of internal fire to keep us going; otherwise, the world would tear us apart too easily. The inner battle between self-destruction and self-preservation wages a unique war. It isn't always easy to choose what side you're on, but then sometimes, fate makes that choice for you.

At the End of the Day I Burst into Flames introduces us to Martin, also known as Firecracker. From the beginning, Martin tells us, "My eyes explode. I feel inferno in my bones, like my father before me. I'll be flame soon enough. I'll be ash shortly after." That striking imagery instantly reeled me in during my first read of Nicholas Day's novella, and it hooked me just as quickly upon revisiting the book. What does it mean, to feel inferno in one's bones?

Martin shows us glances of this, of the fate he knows he cannot escape. The book becomes both a memoir and suicide note for the protagonist. As readers, we're aware of this on an intellectual level pretty early on, but the emotional aspects are written with such authenticity, it becomes impossible not to feel what Martin feels as he continues onward. Death is boiling within this man who has inherited spontaneous combustion in his genetics, and we gather around as spectators to witness his chosen remembrances until the end arrives.

The idea of life flashing before one's eyes in their final moments is nothing new, but what Day accomplishes in the novella goes so much deeper than platitudes. He throws clichés into a wood chopper, and what comes out is a viscerally engaging story told in fragments of past recollections. Day makes sure we are immersed in prose so rich, it feels like a beautiful cocoon come to wrap up the terrible fate Martin will endure. The moments we're privy to in the book are raw and vulnerable. There are memories that make our cheek burns in shame and our hearts race, that lead our minds to recall our own formative experiences of discovering love and how it can soothe and destroy.

Martin contemplates the addiction of it, how the opiate of love both pulls him toward death and away from it: "And I'm not talking about love in some sentimental way. I'm talking about chemical compositions, like if it were possible to put music in a syringe and then stick it in your arm and feel the ebb and flow of notes pulsing through your veins before music takes an aural shit all over your brain." The highs and lows of love, the exhilaration and the anguish, Martin revels in it all, and he knows such a combination seems intent to follow him until the fiery end. With that knowledge, it's no wonder Martin is addicted to love. He will have a finite amount of it in his life. Letting ourselves become close to people in a world where one of us will die first is perhaps one of the scariest aspects of being human.

He also covers the gritty details of his childhood, and doesn't neglect to reminisce on his experiences with getting older, with sexuality, and with identity as a whole. As a reader, I mused over those tales and also realized how much life Martin should have left to live. He could have had decades ahead with his family and friends, with endless possibilities, but that will never be. With lines like "Death, as it turns out, is a librarian of sorts. And he's come to collect my story. I think about love. And I don't want to die," we can't help but want to collect Martin's story, too. We are gluttons for the vividness of his stories; we'll be there until the end, and we know we'll watch him burn.

Martin knows fate is not a thing he can fight. Consider your inevitable final seconds in life. If you had the time, what would you want to think about? What memories would pop into your head, both good and bad? Sometimes we don't want to relive certain hours from the past, but our brain taunts us with those soured events anyway. Martin recalls it all, the times filled with cringing awkwardness and the ones filled with ecstasy. He recalls life, not a dreamy and idyllic recreation of it.

Day's writing, throughout each paragraph, has a sharp way of cutting through any bullshit and exposing the truth of Martin's world. There is a fire there that keeps every moment engaging. All of those sensitive and fascinating flashbacks become splayed out like pinned butterfly wings. There's a sadness captured so delicately in the prose. Each reminiscence is a charm lulling us into its magic through the power of writing. We will walk with Martin in his museum of memories, and we will feel with terrifying realness everything he tells to us. Day succeeds in creating such a personal intimacy through these written recollections, it feels like we're cracking open Martin's skull and reading his most private thoughts. No word is wasted, and it's through such dedication that Day succeeds in creating such a poignant and notable book.

How will you use the fire burning inside your skin? It could consume you, turn you to ashes, but I hope you use your fire to live and dance with blazing abandon until the very moment you no longer can.

AT THE END OF THE DAY I BURST INTO FLAMES

* * *

My eyes explode.

I feel inferno in my bones, like my father before me. I'll be flame soon enough. And I'll be ash shortly after.

I have a story to tell before this happens and *it is* happening soon. Going to be blunt when I want to be. May wander a bit as stories do.

As life does.

And death.

***

In the lateness of a white, Midwest winter, I broke the red door's latch.

Few students, and even less faculty, were present at the high school, as it was well after regular hours. The two of us, she and I, we were part of the high school's freshmen thespian department, painting sets in advance of that year's musical. She was not my girlfriend, only someone I considered a close friend.

Inspiration, the kind inherent to youth, took hold of me and in turn I took hold of her. Up two flights of stairs, quickly and quietly, unobserved and not missed by anyone else. The door was small, the latch was weak, and once broken I led her out onto the rooftop of the school. The lone street lamp may as well have been some meager candlelight.

The sky was black. Snow fell like so much static, cold ash from some unseen fire in Heaven. I taught her the Box Step. I did not know it then, but our intimacy would begin and end with that silent waltz.

Years later, we are separated by decades and decisions, lovers and children. We are separated by life. Our dance is now a memory, fleeting, although the setting remains vivid, as does her smile.

I can no longer remember her name, but I love her.

***

I think about suicide a lot and I think about love.

I think about the fact they we're basically sacks of gooey, communicable chemicals hardwired to survive through sloppy DNA exchange. I think to myself.

It's a system

And any system can be beat if we just fight against what the system wants. I think about suicide and I think that suicide is winning.

But then I remember, individually, we are all dying anyway. It's going to happen. We committed suicide the moment we passed through a membrane from another dimension.

Then, I think.

The system wants us to die

Living is the only way to beat the system.

So, I think about suicide but I don't do it.

Eventually, I come around to the third option, which is that there is no system. Never was. I'm fighting with myself. And that's the one, that's the really depressing revelation. I am my own enemy.

I am the system

I think about love.

Every time I think *yeah . . . okay, I'm going to do it.*

Right?

It's time to finally kill myself. But I almost immediately remember love. And love is so addicting.

Love brings me back.

And I'm not talking about love in some sentimental way. I'm talking about chemical compositions, like if it were possible to put music in a syringe and then stick it in your arm and feel the ebb and flow of notes pulsing through your veins before music takes an aural shit all over your brain.

I'm talking about love-as-opiate.

And I'm so weak, so wrecked and dependent, so addicted, that I can't even fucking kill myself. It's depressing. Love is rubbish. If I could just kick the habit, you know? I'd like to have control over my life.

Of course, I am getting well ahead of myself and this melancholy mindset is due to the fact I am about to die in the same terrible manner as my father, and his father before him, and so on.

I am a lot like my father.

Got the fire inside me.

Time slows to a crawl when Death walks in. We're friends, Death and I. We've met on several occasions but almost always by coincidence, like co-workers who see each other in the parking lot before they go into the big building and do what they do in different rooms, on different floors.

Death, as it turns out, is a librarian of sorts.

And he's come to collect my story.

I think about love.

And I don't want to die.

***

I have a wife and kids. They don't know the fire is coming and I haven't told them. Don't need the ones I love to see me as a ticking clock. No reason to mourn before I'm dead. Can't imagine anything worse than becoming a ghost before it's time. '

Been chewing the inside of my cheek a lot more, lately, that's for sure.

Cigarette is lit and I puff away. Smoke too much. Always have. Should've quit years ago, kick the habit.

Kick the habit

Worthless phrase, really. So easy to say yet so hard to actually do. It isn't like saying, "Kick the dog." You can readily do that . . . given you have a dog and at least one foot.

A habit like smoking may as well be a possession. Got to get a priest if you want a proper exorcism. Want to know how I feel about priests? See if you recognize this quote:

"Fuck the police."

That I temper the anxiety caused by my imminent immolation by lighting up cigarettes is a black humor that isn't entirely lost on me. Fight fire with fire, as my great-great-grandmother had been fond of saying. Lately, though, the smoking has gotten out of hand. Understandably so, given the circumstance.

My wife and I, we're rarely intimate anymore. Emily, God rest her soul. I mean, God rest her soul for putting up with my lacking libido. I don't want to make it look like she's dead. Of course the sex would be bad. And gross. What would the kids think of me if that were the case? I can see Robby's third-grade teacher inquiring about life at our house.

"And how are your parents, Robby?"

To which my brown-eyed, stout son would reply, "Mom is dead but Dad doesn't mind because now they have alone time whenever he wants and Mom never complains."

My son talks like that, you know? Real fast, in exploding sentences. The boy has absolutely no time for a comma in his speech. He will make a great public speaker. I could have been one of those.

***

I came to my hometown of Wood River to reminisce. I actually live in Edwardsville, about an hour's drive southeast. Edwardsville is a lovely town, a college town, actually. The community has a really nice public high school, too, one of the highest rated in Illinois.

But Wood River, that's where my roots are, you know?

Now, maybe, I ought to take a second to set the scene—if you don't mind—to paint a picture in your head, a portrait of the town where I was born and raised and within whose borders I will most certainly die.

First, imagine a metal erector set built by giants. It buzzes with florescent light, belches enough smoke to dwarf the clouds in the sky, and pisses fire so bright that nighttime becomes nothing more than a perpetual evening. Add to that the smell of sulfur. Now, surround this vision with little suburbs full of modest homes, mostly vinyl siding, but pockets of brick in the older neighborhoods. You see green trees, wide yards, lots of trucks and big garages. During the summer, you hear the almost choral hum of a thousand air conditioners working in unison. In the winter, well, I don't really know how it sounds. I stay inside.

It gets too damn cold.

The city is kind of like me in that we both started out as one thing and, over time, we both became something else. You see, Wood River, the part that I grew up in, used to be called Benbow City. At the time, it was hardly more than a green spot on the state border, nothing much more than a humid floodplain along the Mississippi River. Like me, the fire was hidden inside, waiting to be let free.

Then, Standard Oil showed up and that all started to change.

The Wood River Refinery was built in 1907 and, shortly after, a fellow named A.E. Benbow founded his city pretty much right across the street. It wasn't nothing much more than a place to get drunk, gamble, and fuck, but man alive was that town making some money. Once upon a time, Benbow was, *per capita*, the richest city in the whole United States.

Some people called it the wettest town in all of Illinois, one saloon for every thirteen residents. Of course, you can't be making claims like that and not see a significant increase in the population. A stable job, good pay, plenty of places to get a drink and a chance to get laid . . . Benbow was a blue collar's wet dream.

A Wet American Dream.

But, my daddy used to say that if something sounds too good to be true, then it is just that.

By 1917, the party was over in Benbow. In January of that year, the courts found a lady guilty for making prostitutes out of little girls. Couple of months later, the law rounded up a whole bunch of folks for running what they referred to as vice resorts. Then, a couple of days after that, a real popular place called the Red Onion got shut down.

The fun police really cleaned up the joint. By the end of that year, Mayor Benbow gave up. Wood River annexed the place and, like me, Benbow wasn't known by its old name. It was Wood River from there on out. I'd wager to say that more people remember my real name than even know Benbow existed.

Folks around here got a short-term memory when it comes to history. Matter of fact, I find that it's the strangers that seem to know most about the city.

I guess, when you're born in a place, well, you just get to living in it and not thinking about how it all began. Hell, if you weren't standing there and watching it happen, chances are you don't even know about my daddy. Maybe you don't know about the floods either. That was all over the television when it happened. And if you don't know about that stuff, well, then you sure as hell don't know about the fire that swept through downtown in 1912. Shoot, you can't even find old newspaper clippings about that fire. The only reason I know about it is because my great-great-grandma used to go on and on.

"Hell of a fire," she'd say. "Just me and the bucket brigade running around like a bunch of screaming meemies. Terrible thing. Lost my papa to that one."

It seems like, especially in a little old town like this, the stories coming out of old folk's mouths is as close to a history book as a place is apt to get. Sometimes, I look over the obituaries just to lament all the stories I ain't never gonna hear, because if you never heard some these old fart's stories, then those stories were going to the grave, like every obit is a little piece of history getting buried up at Woodlawn Cemetery.

And that's that, I guess. I grew up there. I went to Wood

River High, married the homecoming queen, had a future.

Now I smoke, my homecoming queen is getting older, and my future? Well, I have a semi-lucrative job drawing raunchy cartoons for top-of-the-line porno magazines. You'd know the cartoons if you saw them: Jokes about old men's balls and lady's sagging breasts; Santa getting it on with Mrs. Claus with mood lighting provided by Rudolph; Cute, furry animals using foul language.

And I meant what I said about semi-lucrative. The money is surprisingly good. I have an art studio in the basement of our house, so I get to work at home. Send out this comic to that magazine and this comic out to that magazine.

I'm terribly popular at porn conventions. Young kids, mostly boys, seem to really get a kick out of my work. "Funny shit," they'll say.

"Thanks," I'll say. And I'll usually wave my hand in appreciation. I make sure I never shake hands with anyone. It is a porn convention, after all.

But I am getting ahead of myself.

The first thing I ought to tell you about is how my daddy burst into flames when I was six years old.

***

Dad caught the fire just before my seventh birthday.

The doctors called it nothing. They didn't have a name for what happened, except accident, which, *goddamn*, I guess so. But my momma had a name for it and she called it spontaneous combustion.

Mom said the fire was an Act of God, and if you know anything about God then you know damn well that God doesn't go making accidents on people, so those doctors were just plain wrong, or maybe not right with the Lord. Maybe, she reckoned, all that control they thought they had over life and death made them a little punch drunk, a little jealous, like if they kept doctoring long enough and came up with enough names for medicines and maladies that maybe, just maybe, well, maybe they could beat God.

Then be God.

But before I even get into Daddy and all that, I think maybe you ought to know that my daddy's daddy burned up the very same way.

Just poof and flame then gone.

Now I didn't see grandpa light up—just my daddy—but my daddy and mom saw gramps go. Daddy hated talking about it, but he would, occasionally, and usually when he was plenty liquored up. Mom, though, she would talk about it every Sunday, sometimes taking her time with the story and other times telling it in a rush of a couple sentences.

The ending was always the same.

Mom would look up to the sky, in sun or snow or rain or whatever God was throwing down.

"He was like a firecracker," she'd whisper. "Just like a firecracker."

She must have liked the word, the way the consonants clicked and clacked in the back of her mouth, because it eventually became her pet name for me.

Firecracker.

Damn if that name didn't stick with anyone in an earshot. And earshot is a pretty easy thing to be in a little town like Wood River. By the time Daddy died, well, I ceased being whoever I was and, instead, I became Firecracker.

***

Downtown Wood River is a sad affair. Empty storefront windows are the ghosts of past prosperity. Even worse is when those windows are broken or boarded over, as if faded glories were too exhausting to take care of.

I finish my cigarette and head down the road to The Night Cap, a tavern that used to be little more than a dive bar but ended up being bought out by some entrepreneurial spirit who changed it into . . . a dive bar with a patio.

My allergies act up, and when I go to rub my nose I notice the way my hand smells like stale nicotine. I shove my hand in my pocket, punishing it for my own bad habit, forcing it to play endlessly with change. Should've quit years ago.

Not that it will matter in a couple of hours.

I walk through Night Cap's front door. It smells like forty years of spilled drinks, with just a hint of disinfectant and diluted bleach. Thankfully, a single window and dim lighting help mask the rest.

Night Cap has a respectable menu for a greasy spoon. The Italian stuff is pretty tasty, but I'm too wound up for a plate of solid food. What I want is a cheap, cold beer.

I coast past the pool tables and the pock-marked dart board and make my way to the back of the place. A lack of clientele surprises me. I remind myself that it is Tuesday afternoon.

People have things to do besides drink a dozen or so beers while they await the inevitable.

All the tables in the back of Night Cap are the same. Round tables, wood laminate tops, each surrounded by four chairs. Ketchup, salt, pepper, and sugar sit in their centers. I glance over each table, as though it is some kind of hard decision as to where I'll put my ass. Even worse, I already know which seat I'll take. But I still act out the decision-making process. It is a habit. I do this every time I come here.

Finally, I very casually make my way to the table where I proposed to Emily.

***

"You know what? You can tell the level of a person's anxiety by the length of their fingernails." And I held up my hand to show her.

The first time I'd ever worked up the courage to speak to Emily.

Senior year of high school, for sure, so I'd have been seventeen. In an elevator that broke down, getting nervous, and sitting between the second and third floor of the high school's main building. We were both running late to class, though that didn't really matter at that point. Class would be over long before the fire department would get us out.

I sucked at math anyway.

Emergency lights glowed and colored the elevator's insides in deep red. Heard voices, faculty, I guessed, but they sounded a million miles away. Everything will be all right was their mantra.

The air inside the elevator bunched up your underwear and made your t-shirt feel one size too tight. Not the kind of warm that makes you sweat, it just made you uncomfortable. The red lights didn't help, either; it looked like we were in an oven.

Or in Hell.

I thought about my morning, thought about homework, missed classes, anything other than broken elevators.

Emily had a kindness. Always first to say hello in the halls. She would hold a door open for you, even if her own hands were full. Emily, quick to joke, loved puns, though I rarely heard her laugh. Instead, she smiled. The better a joke the wider her smile, until her brown eyes were hardly visible. I felt very relaxed around her, even though I didn't have the nerve to approach her. To my young senses, Emily had a kind of perfection usually reserved for dreams, like the hum of something fantastic.

You see, by this point, my addiction to love had already taken hold of me but my supplier was long gone. I needed a fix. Emily was my clumsy attempt to get high.

"You shouldn't chew on your nails," Emily told me. "It's a bad habit."

She was right and I know I blushed. My embarrassment went thankfully unnoticed. Red lights made all other shades obsolete.

People kept going on outside the elevator shaft. They tried to put us at ease, I suppose, but they sounded anxious. I decided to drown them out.

Then, I spaced out looking at that red light and I thought about a boy named Stephen.

***

I had known Stephen since grade school. An awkward kid, but super smart, and always wore the same red sweatshirt when we were very little. He looked like a big candy apple and I told him that, once. He kicked me in the balls. First time we'd really interacted.

The second time was also the last day he lived in my neighborhood.

Stephen shared the house across the street with his mom. His parents never married but his dad would come around every once in a while. This was back when my dad was still alive.

Stephen and I rode the same school bus and we would make the same walk home every day. Neither of us was too fond of one another. I thought Stephen to be nothing but a chubby, weird dork. He thought I acted like an insensitive moron. We didn't know anything about each other, but we never really made the effort, so we would just glare at one another.

Every once in a while we'd mutter insults under our breath.

To irritate him, I walked on his side of the street, which forced him to walk on my side of the street. I loved doing this because I knew that he'd eventually have to cross over in order to get to his mom's house. When we crossed paths, we'd enact our little ritual.

As soon as Stephen walked in an earshot, I uttered a very soft, "Bitch."

To which Stephen would reply, "Asshole."

The exchange enabled us to remind each other that we were there and we existed.

I let my eyes wander to Stephen and tried to anticipate when he would cross and I saw something that I initially thought looked like garbage all heaped together at the end of Stephen's driveway. But it wasn't garbage day and what I saw wasn't bags. It was clothes.

A body lay by the road in front of Stephen's house. The body had been his mother.

I dropped my books and turned toward Stephen. The clatter caught his attention. He looked at me and then beyond me and I could see the change in his expression. His eyes widened, mouth drooped into an ugly frown and that quickly became a scream. He flung his books to the street and he ran to his home. I held out a hand, as if I could grab all his pain and yank it away from existence.

I couldn't hear Stephen's screams.

I couldn't hear anything at all.

Sound had disappeared. I'm not entirely sure I was even in my own body. I had become a camera, a simple observer to an event for which I had no way to compartmentalize.

Every moment slowed down and drew out to such a length that I could literally see between the seconds.

Time grinded to a halt like ancient clockwork.

Darkness and light became as a curtain, which rippled and pulled apart to reveal a human shape whose eyes shone like dying stars and whose clothes were fashioned from shadow and fog.

Death looked at me from the void outside of time.

He held his palms outward, as if this body and the boy's grief were a gift to me.

The ghost of Stephen's mother peered at me through the black folds of Death's cloak, and then the specter retreated from reality, back through the curtain of light and illusion.

Time returned to normal and I heard mournful sobs like gasps of air.

A chubby little boy rocked his mother in an obscene reversal of their relationship up to that point. Stephen cried so much that his mother's hair had dampened. An image of my own mother rocking me and singing a lullaby comforted me for all but a brief moment. Stephen's lullaby articulated itself by way of streaming tears, screams and pleas for help.

Stephen's wailing sounded like a heart breaking forever.

And I ran to him.

The trees were just sprouting leaves, some more developed than others, but still enough to shade us from the sun. Stephen threw his arms around me and I put my arms around him. Neighbors started coming out of their homes to see about all the commotion.

Dad marched out into the street. He heard Stephen screaming and figured we were fighting. Like he and Momma would fight.

Sometimes I could hear them through the walls. Always at night. They thought I was asleep.

Dad told me Stephen's mother succumbed to the heat and she

died exerting herself. Stephen moved into his father's house that evening.

I felt Stephen's fingers as though they were pressed into my back the whole night. I thought of him as a ghost and never realized how often he would return to my life and haunt me.

That's when the bad dreams began. Nightmares about men made of fire.

And the terror of seeing between the seconds where Death watched and waited.

***

His legs were thick as his arms, like hams you'd see in the deli window at Christmas. He had height at his disposal, always looking down, always imposing. But there was a smile, and his eyes would disappear and you knew you were safe. His voice was deep and when he picked you up, the grip had the same foundation as the ground below. His skin was cheap soap in the morning, salty musk and oil at the end of a hard day. He made me small, insignificant.

I felt like his whole way of being was as a mountain to climb and I was unprepared for the journey, set up from birth to fail him, and thus fail myself. As a child, he had been God Above, but now he was a man, rough around the edges and used, a blunt instrument that was well-loved and then forgotten, replaced by something newer, more efficient, but somehow less.

"I have the fire inside me," he said, smoke billowing from the cuffs and collar of his shirt.

He burst into flames.

And he reached for me.

This is the dream, and I have it often.

***

Emily and I dated at the end of high school and when high school ended we dated in college. I'd lost love twice by then and was bound and determined not to lose it a third time. Ours was a courthouse wedding.

I took a freelance gig for school credit that turned into a full-time illustrating position and I proposed to Emily after graduation. We married the following summer. She landed a teaching position.

Emily educates second graders at Collinsville Middle School, just outside of Edwardsville. A grade school teacher, she's the yin to my yang. I make more money but she gets better benefits. I know it sounds resentful, but with two kids we could use the extra cash.

Our oldest, Brandon, is in high school. He *doesn't* smoke. Brandon plays football. He's a quarterback at Edwardsville High School. I tried to get him interested in art and even writing but neither stuck. He's too much like his mother.

Emily and I go to all of Brandon's games. He plays really well, I think. Emily was a sports fanatic when we were younger. She played softball for Wood River. I would go to see her games, smoking habitually in the stands. Emily says Brandon plays well, and I believe her.

I think Brandon is homosexual. I brought this up to Emily last night. My hope was that Brandon would come out to us, though it didn't look like that was going to happen.

Unfortunately, at this point my time was running short and I felt like I needed to say something before I was gone for, well . . . forever.

"Honey, you ever think Bran is different?" I lowered my glasses to let her know I was serious.

Emily had just come up from the laundry room; a full basket crammed under one arm. She dumped the clothes on our bed and turned toward me.

"Why in the hell would you of all people worry about him being different?"

"He's never had a girlfriend, for one."

"But he's only—"

"Seventeen, Em. Yes, I *am* aware of his age."

"He's a shy boy." Emily balled her hands into fists and rested them on her hips. I could see her working the inside of her cheek. She took a defensive stance, though I had no idea at that time what she had to be so defensive about.

"Okay," I said. "Why does he play sports if he's so shy?"

"He says it's out of habit." She turned away from me and toward the laundry. "He's not gay, if that's what you're thinking."

"You mean you asked him about it?"

"Months ago."

"So *you* think he's gay?"

"No." She threw a pair of folded socks which smacked me in the chest. "Look, I get it. You didn't have a good father figure in your life, so you're trying to fill that hole, but you're just being paranoid."

Emily edged close to the truth. Paranoid, yes, but not because I wanted to fill some hole left in my life by my father. I knew my end approached even if Emily did not.

I had seen the fire in all its glory.

***

Dad died within days of my seventh birthday.

Mom used to wait outside for me when I got home from school. I loved to see her wave from the lawn. I used to think she waited for me outside because she hated me fighting with Stephen but he was gone and she was still there and still waiting. Mom always told me fighting's no good and that I ought not get into fights with other boys and especially not to fight with girls. She said it wasn't nice and that it hurt their feelings. Mom once told me how to tell if a girl has been upset.

Look at her fingernails. Happy girls always have long, pretty nails.

Mom had very nice nails that she kept painted red, but they never went past the tip of her finger.

Sometimes I heard her cry.

I had asked my dad what was wrong. He would say that she had fallen down, or that she had burned herself with the curling iron, or that she had bit her lip. Dad slept in the living room some nights.

Sometimes, Dad would come home and say awful things to Mom. He bullied her into their room and I could hear them shouting. I listened to them for a long time. One night, Dad came into my bedroom. The room was dark and he was silhouetted against the hallway light. He crossed his arms and leaned against the door. I smelled something sour in the air. He came over to my bed and sat down. I think he was crying.

He was a big guy, my old man, so when he sat on my bed I rolled right into him. He stroked my hair. I saw his face clearly. He looked at me, his lips quivered. A trickle of snot ran from his nose and he breathed through his mouth. He raised his hand and I thought he would hit me.

"Can't stop what's coming, son." He clenched his fist tight and his arm trembled. He stared up at the ceiling. Don't know what he saw but I like to think he was angry at God and not me.

Dad put his hand down. He kissed my forehead. I fell asleep shortly after he left the room.

The next morning, we gathered in the kitchen. No snow on the ground outside but I remember frost and it was real heavy, like the Good Lord saw fit to cover the earth in cellophane. Dad wore nothing but a pair of briefs and I am almost dead certain that he complained about the heat, because I remember thinking how strange it was that anybody could complain of heat when their breath hung in the air like tiny clouds.

I mean we weren't exactly rolling in dough back then. The heat in the house stayed off until the first snowfall of the year. So, even though I could see a breath in the air, well, that still wasn't snow on the ground.

"Grab a blanket. Sit in the kitchen," Daddy would say, and he'd turn on the oven, letting the heavy metal door sit open just a hair.

I'll tell you what, that oven made a pretty swell fireplace.

We had some good times in that kitchen, huddled together and wearing blankets and playing cards or telling stories.

Mornings in that kitchen, like we were at camp. Hell, that was some thirty-odd years ago, but even now I am inclined to go into my own kitchen and turn on the oven before I even think of running up the thermostat.

I remember Daddy saying something like, "It's hotter than blue blazes in here."

Momma and I sat at the kitchen table already bundled up in our blankets and when he said that, well, I had to look at him to see if he was joking around.

That's when I realized he was steaming. Not the angry kind —mind you—but really steaming, like a pot left to boil too long.

Momma said, "Maybe you ought to sit down, baby."

I don't recall Dad walking over to the table as much as I can remember the sound of his feet on the linoleum floor. Every step made an ugly little sucking sound, like his feet were sticking to the ground.

He looked wet, like slick plastic, like a Halloween costume. And he still steamed after he sat, but he wasn't sweating. I guess, in retrospect, it must have been too damn hot to sweat.

Our last exchange went a little something like this:

I said, "Dad, you feeling bad?

"I feel a might bit funny," he said, and then his eyes burst out of his head. "Oh shit."

Daddy burst into flames.

Momma started screaming, "Baby, baby, baby," over and over and louder and louder.

I sat there like a bump on a log.

Momma beat and whipped Daddy with her blanket but the blanket offered no help. That fire wasn't going out. Daddy finally got up and pushed her away from him.

He ran through the house all ablaze, running into walls and doors and furniture. I figured he must have been looking for a way out. Momma couldn't do much more than sit on the floor and scream every time he hit something, so I started yelling out directions for him.

"Go left, Daddy!"

"Watch out for the ottoman!"

"Watch out for the chair!"

"Put out your hands! That's the pie safe you're touching."

And once he knew that he was standing in front of the pie safe, well, blind or not, the man knew that house pretty well. He was at the front door lickety-split and then out into the yard. Momma picked herself up and went following. So did I except I didn't scream like she did.

Daddy kind of stumbled a bit outside and for some reason he started over towards the neighbor lady's place. The frost melted before him like a crowd separated for a great man, or the way folks in westerns used to back out of the streets when there was going to be a gunfight. He fell right in front of the door to the neighbor lady's house, and that's when the fire became too much for his body to hold.

Now, it was real strange, but when Daddy was bouncing around our house he never once lit anything else on fire. Maybe he left a smudge of burnt skin here and there, and of course his hair went up quick and smelled something awful, but nothing caught, nothing went up along with him.

That changed right quick, though, and fire belched out from his fallen body and started eating away at Ms. Mackeninny's house.

With Ms. Mackeninny inside.

I'll tell you, I thought Momma was screaming to beat the band, but man oh man did Mackeninny make a racket.

That's about the time all the neighbors came out to see the fuss, to see the greatest fire they'd ever seen.

Mackeninny stopped screaming long before the fire department showed up.

I watched them hook their great big hose to the hydrant up the street. They came running up the yard and they were ready to blast the house with a horizontal waterfall. When they pulled the valve, that hose farted out a trickle of water about as powerful as my showerhead. Back then it was awful intense, but I have to admit it's kind of funny to me now.

Daddy used to tell me that, when it came time, I ought not to worry about a fancy funeral or anything like that.

"Don't put me in no box, either," he'd say, and then Momma would get so mad.

"You don't want to be buried next to me?" She'd ask.

"I don't want to be buried at all," he'd reply.

"You don't love me." She'd say.

"It has nothing to do with loving you," he'd say. "I want to be cremated is all."

"Fine, be cremated. But if you go before me then I'm just having your ashes dumped in my grave." And that's about the time in the argument where she'd stick out her chin and nod her head as if it were the period at the end of a sentence.

"Ah, goddammit." And that is what Dad would say when the argument had ended.

Momma stayed true to her word. After the fire, we scooped up whatever we thought might have been Dad and we put it in two different envelopes.

"This'll be buried with me," she said and handed me the second envelope, adding, "and you can take this with you."

So, that's it, really, about my daddy. He burned up and that's that. Momma and her envelope are already in the grave. My envelope is locked away in a safety deposit box that'll be popped open sometime very soon.

But did I see Death when the old man went up in flames?

Surely I did, though not at that exact moment.

Death came to me like he comes to us all, in sleep, when we enter his Library of Lives.

***

I am tied to a chair and my mother won't stop putting food into my mouth and she keeps feeding and feeding me and then I realize she is feeding me the remains of my father and, my God, it's delicious. I eat every bite of him, right down to the bone. Then, my grandmother, my father's mother, comes into the kitchen but she's naked and walking around like she used to do when she thought everyone was still asleep. She helps my mother crush up Dad's bones until they're nothing but a powder.

They cut up the powdered bone into lines.

"Do you like skiing?" my mother asks. The two of them start snorting the powder and laughing.

My stomach begins churning and growling. Not because I'm sick but because Dad is so angry. I can feel him inside of me, moving in my guts. It's the pain that makes you double over, as if a cue ball is pushing its way through your intestine and that ball has at least seven feet of tight, coiled rollercoaster left before the ride stops.

I have to get to a bathroom, I think. Dad is so awful when he's angry but I am still tied to a chair and I can't get up. The pain is terrible. I start trying to jerk loose but the rope won't come undone. I start sweating and I am afraid I might shit myself, so I begin to shimmy my pants off. Now, my trousers are at my knees and I am bouncing in my chair, which falls over and that pressure in my gut, that cue ball, it finally reaches my asshole while I am face down on the ground.

I'm pinching so tight that if I did fart it would probably sound like I was whistling a song, and as that thought crosses my mind I laugh and the pressure explodes into something as orgasmic as it is nauseating, but instead of a fart, all I can hear is my father hollering, screaming excrement all over my mother, his mother, and everything else in the kitchen.

***

I wake up shivering and crying the night before my death, a full-grown man reduced to childhood emotion. Everyone is asleep and it is dark, but I cover my face anyway, thinking that if God is real then I would rather not have him see me like this. I am ashamed, not because of the dream but because I only sat and watched while Dad died in front of me. I was never tied down in real life, though I sat at the table all the same, like a good boy.

Dad was so awful when he was angry, just like God, and if God is real and he sees me covering my face then I have no doubt that God knows why I am crying. And if God knows then Dad knows because He would have told him, because that's what happens when you die, that's the consolation for having lived a mortal life. All secrets are set free. I am covering my face because Dad is so angry at me. I am afraid that if I take my hand down and open my eyes that I will see him in the dark.

"Go away," I sob. "Please, go away."

Soon, I fall asleep, exhausted, having shed as many tears as one can, and with a throbbing headache, too. Throb, throb, tic, toc. The pounding in my heart is making clockwork in my head and it is awfully painful. My last coherent thought, the one I'll remember in the morning just before I open my eyes for the first time, is that my headache sounds so much like my father's booming footsteps. And with that realization comes a deep sleep and another dream.

My father is trapped inside his own graven image. He strips away from the inside out. He is free and violent and hungry. Nothing can stop him, nothing can stop me, and we are both on fire.

I wake up very early on the day I die and decide that if I am to burn, then it won't be in front of my family. I'll go away, anywhere, as long as it is far from them. The fire is my burden.

***

I found a frog smashed into the pavement right before I fell in love for the second time. His blue and purple guts squeezed out like a crunched-up bunch of shoelace. His pink tongue pressed out of green lips and bent over on itself, as if it got tired of hanging out the mouth. Being dead looked exhausting and wet.

Could crushed frogs haunt pavement?

"Hey, frog," I whispered. "Do you have a soul?"

I waited, though the frog said nothing. The other kids at the bus stop watched me. An older boy, some nameless kid whose voice fluctuated between tenor and bass, he pointed right at me.

"Are you talking to a dead frog?"

"No." I said.

"You're that weirdo kid that falls down and shakes in class."

"I'm not weird."

"I heard you pee your pants when it happens."

"Leave him alone," said a voice from behind me.

It was Stephen. He lived in a different neighborhood, now, but still rode the same bus. We never gave each other any grief after his mom died. Once, Stephen cradled me while I had a seizure on the playground. He didn't have to do that.

We both stared at that frog. It was another minute or two before Stephen finally spoke up.

"I'm sorry about the frog."

The bus pulled up. We got on, sat next to each other and

didn't say a word. Stephen held my hand.

He didn't have to do that, but I'm glad he did.

***

Every hour we changed class, and every hour I thought about that frog. I looked at a lot of faces, looked into people's eyes and spied on their souls, listened to the slips and wisps of tongues on lips and teeth, but never once did I forget that frog. Never once did time slow down, never once did I see a shadowy figure step out of the folds of time. Bad thoughts and balled fists were offered here and there from bullies, but nasty as those things may be, they weren't really any interest to me, so I ignored them.

And I thought about death.

"You're not still thinking about that frog, are you?" Stephen asked me during lunch.

I shook my head. "I see it everywhere I look."

"What is it about a dead frog, anyway?"

I looked at Stephen. I saw his mother standing in his eyes. She smiled at me. Her teeth were too white, too big, too many. Her skin looked like it fit all wrong. Something moved beneath her flesh. Stephen opened his mouth but all that came out was a scream.

It was my fault. My eyes had rolled up and my body shook. I think he held me.

I think he held me till I fell asleep.

***

It wasn't the first time I woke up in the nurse's office. Mamma sat beside me. Her hands cupped mine.

"Are you okay, Firecracker?"

"Mamma, do frogs have souls?"

She drew her hands away and held them in her lap. She looked at me, opened her mouth as if to say something. Her face filled with color and she put a hand over her mouth. I thought she was going to cry. Her color, her real color, came back. It was a funny kind of smile.

"Whatever made you ask that question?"

"I had a strange dream."

"Dreams aren't real, baby. Dreams are all in your head."

"Are nightmares real?"

She laid her hand on my chest. "Stop," she said. "Just stop."

I saw the disappointment and I looked away. Mamma hardly looked at me like that, like I wasn't her son. I may as well have been a stranger that had stolen her love, and I was so scared that she would ask for it back. Mamma meant the world to me. Of course she had no answers to give to me. That didn't stop me. I took a hold of her hand.

"If you had a soul, Mamma, you could give it to me and I'll take it away."

Mamma stood up. She looked across the room, and for the first time, I realized that the nurse sat only a few feet away from us. The face she made at Mamma was something else. Mamma just waved a hand at the lady and shook her head.

"He's fine, just a little delirious from the episode."

"Right," said the nurse.

"Come on, Firecracker. We're going home."

I got in Momma's bright-red van and she played "Vanished" by Crystal Castles on repeat, all the way home. She did that a lot, played the songs she loved over and over. I tried to imagine what she'd look like on fire and the thought gave me a shiver. What kind of music would a fire listen to on repeat?

I didn't want to find out.

***

Sunrise was streaks of warm color and birdsong. The wind chime on our back porch betrays the silent breeze and its music follows me as I walk back into the house and tip toe inside. I leave the door open. The breeze gently haunts the kitchen curtains and the tablecloth.

I make a cup of coffee just as quietly as I can but it's not for me. It's for Emily. I put in two scoops of sugar because I know that she likes it sweet. The breeze pushes in much harder than before and stirs up all the comforting scents of the house and our life. I take a deep breath and then a second one. This time I close my eyes.

It is the last time I'll ever be in this house. I can't stay here anymore. I don't want them to see the fire. I may have to hide in the woods or in an abandoned building downtown or somewhere near the Mississippi, though none of that troubles me because all I need to do is think about Emily. And think of Stephen. They are all the pleasure I have ever known.

And then I think of the Box Waltz and the snow. A perfect moment. What was her name?

The coffee steams as I place the cup atop Emily's nightstand. The chimes continue but I drown them out by closing the door to our room. She stirs when I sit on the bed and startles when I lightly shake her from the deep sleep. I gently cup her mouth and put a finger to my lips. Her eyes focus on me and she slowly moves my hand away to show that she understands.

"What are you doing?" she whispered.

"I'm heading to Wood River," I said. "Need to run some errands. But I didn't want to leave without saying I love you."

51

***

Stephen had been in and out of mental health facilities for years, and that was well before his mother died. He told me he was a bit violent as a toddler, but it wasn't the violence that landed him a permanent seat in the local psychiatrist's office. It had been his silence. He told me once that his parents suspected a severe learning disability, that even the doctors thought so, on account of the fact that he barely spoke a word the first five years of his life. Not that you'd know it now.

Stephen speaks a lot. To me, at any rate. His voice is soft, as if he's talking you off of a ledge or something, and the way he says stuff, well, you hear it all, every syllable. Perfect pronunciation.

Turned out he didn't bother speaking because he was too busy thinking. It was all numbers, he told me. Numbers was his first language. He could do long division in his head before the words mommy or daddy passed his lips. He was so good at math that the rest of us kids just couldn't compete, and pretty soon the teachers at school figured out that they couldn't compete either. They were afraid of him. Us kids were too stupid to be afraid, and it was easy to think Stephen was just some big dork, but one day our math teacher, Mrs. Clark, decided to see just how smart he was, and after that we stopped thinking of Stephen as one of us.

I mean, he looked like one of us, sure, but he was operating on a different level. Kids, like dogs, can smell fear; it's how bullies choose their marks. Imagine, then, what it was like to recognize that Mrs. Clark wasn't just afraid of Stephen, but terrified of him. To a bunch of squirrelly kids, teachers were practically our parents for eight hours every day of the week, a bunch of omnipotent beings that demanded homework, respect and subordination.

And then, one day, Mrs. Clark asked Stephen to recite his multiplication tables.

"Where do you want me to start?" he asked.

"You can start at the beginning. One through twelve, please."

"How about I start at eighty-two?"

"Please, do as you're told Stephen."

"One hundred sixty-four. Two hundred forty-six. Three hundred twenty-eight. Four hundred ten."

"That's enough, young man."

"Four hundred ninety-two. Five hundred seventy-four—"

"You can stop showing off, please."

Stephen stood up and continued, louder than before.

"Six hundred fifty-six. Seven hundred thirty-eight."

"Sit down immediately."

But Stephen wasn't having any of that, and he kept talking and started walking to the front of the class.

"Eight hundred twenty. Nine hundred two. Nine hundred eighty-four. Want me to go back to one or start at twelve and do it backwards? One hundred forty-four. One hundred thirty-two. One hundred twenty—"

"Stop it this instant and return to your seat."

"I know my multiplication tables. I could do them forever."

"Do you want a detention? Is that what you want?"

"How much do you know about numbers, Mrs. Clark?"

"We are all learning our multiplication tables this week."

"No." He pointed to us. "They're learning how to memorize. That's not math. I didn't learn how to read by memorizing a book."

"I think you need to go to the office. Go to the principal's office immediately."

"You're no smarter than any of us."

"How dare you?" Mrs. Clark stood up. "*You* . . . you just wait right here young man, you wait here and I'll get the principal myself." And she shuffled out of the room and into the hallway, her heels clacking the tile and echoing down the cavernous maw of Wood River High School.

"You're in trouble." I said.

"No I'm not."

"She's going to get Mr. Matthews and he's going to give you a detention."

"Fuck him."

All the kids sucked in and froze, a collective gasp for the reigning king of dirty words.

"Holy cow," somebody whispered. "He said the f-word."

"I want to show you guys something." Stephen grabbed a piece of chalk and drew a circle, a perfect one, on the board. "Do any of you know anything about infinity?"

I raised my hand. "Infinity means forever and ever."

Stephen smiled.

"That's right," he said. "Did you know that the roundness of a circle gets smaller when the circle gets bigger? And I mean lots bigger."

"Like a house?"

"Like a planet. Like the earth. It's round. You look outside across that field as far as you can." Twenty kids craned their necks. I was the only one that got up and went to the window.

"See? It looks flat. We're so tiny and it's so big it looks flat. But it's just a great big circle."

"The bigger the circle gets the flatter it looks?" I asked.

"Because we're so small," he said. "Now, imagine the universe."

"Is the universe round?"

"I think it is. But it's also infinite. So the circle would be so big, so enormous, that all it would look like is a straight line. That's an infinite circle."

"An infinite circle is a straight line."

Stephen laughed, and then I smiled and I laughed because right then and there I knew that Stephen didn't think I was stupid. Maybe he thought that way about the other kids, but not me. I surprised him, and it made me feel good.

One of the kids in the class mumbled, "You guys are crazy." Stephen looked over them and I could see his lips pulling back. He zeroed in, he knew who insulted us. His teeth clenched. He walked over to a chubby kid named Mark, a kid whose baby fat would turn into the muscles of a high school quarterback, a kid that would date cheerleaders and get A's, a kid that bullied me in junior high but thought so little of me that by the time we got to high school he just pretended like I wasn't there. I always hated Mark, even before I really knew him.

Stephen slapped him across the face.

Principal Matthews and Mrs. Clark came rushing in and Mr. Matthews grabbed Stephen and pulled him out of the room. For most of the kids, that was the last time they would see Stephen, but that was the day he and I became best friends, and, now that I think about it, I guess we were always best friends.

The school board decided to give Stephen a test to see how smart he was and after that year they moved him up to the senior level. He told me that he'd begun taking math classes at the local college, but he didn't call them classes, he called them courses. High school kids were dicks, he said, but the college kids were alright because they mostly ignored him. After that year, the high school arranged for Stephen to receive his diploma early. He was a college freshman at fifteen.

"Man, I wish I was in college," I said.

"It's all the same shit, dude. Crappy teachers that barely know more than the students and students that hardly even try to learn. It's like they're robots. Like they're going through life with their switch turned off. They may as well be asleep."

"It's got to be better than high school. I bet there are some hot girls."

"Old ladies you mean? Yuck. You can have them."

"You mean you don't even think about it?"

"I think of everything."

"I'm talking about girls, stupid. Not math. Not the universe."

"I miss being able to hang out at school."

"You never really hung out at school, Stephen."

"I hung out with you."

"Well, yeah, but we still hang out."

"I've been accepted to another university. They want to give me a full scholarship."

"What school?"

"*Schools*. Massachusetts Institute of Technology and Harvard."

"Fuck, dude, those are, like, on the other side of the country."

"I'll be back for the summers."

"Yeah, no, that's cool. I'm sorry. I guess I keep forgetting that you're so far ahead of us. I'm stuck here for another three years. Three years. God I wish I was smart like you."

"You're plenty smart, Firecracker."

"Not like you, dude. You're going to be king of the world."

"I'll just give power over to you. You're better with people than I am."

"If you make me king, then first thing we're going to do is burn this town to the ground. It fucking sucks, dude."

Stephen hugged me. I thought it went on a little too long but then I realized he was crying and I let him hang on until he was done.

"Everything happens for a reason," he said.

And then he went home.

That week, Stephen decided to go to Massachusetts, and he was there by the weekend. We wouldn't speak again until the next year. By that point, I'd danced in the snow and said goodbye to love for the first time, and the addiction had its claws in me.

***

Sophomore year of high school wasn't so bad. Not like the fantasy junk that you see in movies and television. It was a small community. Most of us went to the same schools since we were little kids. Hell, most of our parents went to the very same high school when they were kids. It was like that. Everybody knew everybody by the time we got there. The social order was decided long ago. No need for hazing. No use trying to fit in where you didn't already belong. There was no need for pissing contests. In retrospect, it was like a microcosm of our future.

I could sit back and see future teachers, stay-at-home moms, truck drivers, the local politicians and the criminals. It's like the town knew what you needed to be. I began to think that's why it pushed out Stephen. The town knew he didn't belong. He was the square peg to this town's round hole. It was so perfectly laid out that these kids might as well have gone out to the cemetery and buried themselves. Their fates were written. They were already dead.

Infinite circle, and all that, I guess.

I got a letter from Stephen during Christmas break:

Firecracker,

MIT is amazing. I've found some actual living and breathing humans out here. My age is a novelty, I think. Some of the teachers are put off by how young I am, but at least I can talk to them and they understand me. Math is a real language here.

How is high school? Is Mark still an insufferable ass? Sorry. Rhetorical question, I'm sure.

I wish you could be here, but summer will come soon enough. There is a guy named Eric who lives in my dormitory and loves horror movies. He has people over every Thursday night. I can't wait to show you some of these. They're so gross. Have you heard of Dead Alive?

Look forward to hearing from you.
Stephen

I never sent him a letter. I think part of me was jealous because my life was so boring, so average in comparison, and all I could think to tell him was that I missed him. I began to write:

Stephen,
I miss having you around.

Then I stared at the page for a long, long time. It was such a naked statement. I tried to think of something else to say but it was the truth. Every other thing that went through my brain just sounded meaningless. Or mean. I wanted to blame him for leaving, that no one talked to me. That I was alone and it was his fault. That he was really living. His life was becoming an adventure that I couldn't begin to understand. I wanted to rail at him that the town didn't want him. That it spit him out but it kept me. That it wanted me.

That I wanted to kill myself.

Those words never went to paper. Instead, I tried to forget him, but summer was coming.

Stephen showed up at my house on a warm day in June. In his hand was a stack of DVDs. He didn't say hello. There was no hug. There was only a question:

"Want to watch some horror movies?" he asked.

"What do you got?"

"Alright. I have Night of the Living Dead, Zombie, Dead Alive, Dawn of the Dead, and Let Sleeping Corpses Lie."

"I saw Dawn of the Dead."

"The remake?"

"That was a remake?"

"This one is from the 70s."

"Oh, okay, so which one do you want to watch?"

"As many as we can get through."

"We got to wait till they're asleep."

"Fine by me. We can shoot the shit until they pass out."

Night came quickly. My mom and stepdad went to bed. Stephen said we should watch the films in chronological order. He said it would be better that way. Let it build, he told me. Except, he didn't say build, he said crescendo.

"Let the gore crescendo until it blows your mind."

We were about forty-five minutes into Zombie, that scene where the woman gets her eye taken out by a piece of jagged wood, when I realized Stephen was masturbating beside me in the dark. I didn't dare look at him. He said nothing. There was only the repetitive sound of skin on skin and the occasional sharp breath.

"Look at me." He said.

"Fuck off."

He grabbed me by the shoulder. I turned and punched him in the face. Stephen yelped. He put his hands up to his nose and fell backwards onto the floor, his erection resting against his exposed thigh. I ran to the bathroom and locked myself inside.

There was a light tap, tap, tap on the door.

"I'm sorry. Please. Don't be mad. I didn't mean to freak you out."

My legs were shaking. I sat on the floor.

"Firecracker, how come you never wrote me back?"

I started to cry. "I tried. I really did. But what do you care? You were off fucking around in mathland while I sat here by myself in this shithole. I didn't want to write you, I didn't want to have to. I just wanted you to be around, you know? I guess I felt like if I wrote you that I'd have to admit you were really gone. Like really, really gone. You're my best friend, dickhead, and you left me."

"I think you busted my nose."

"Good."

"Unlock the door so I can use the sink. I don't want to get blood everywhere."

I got up and opened the door. Stephen stood in the dark

hallway, blood running from both nostrils and his green eyes wet with tears. The low-fi sound of badly dubbed actors being torn apart by zombies murmured quietly from my room. I looked away from him.

"It's okay," he said. "It doesn't hurt."

I backed up a little to give him clear passage to the sink. But he didn't go to the sink. He walked right up to me. I still couldn't look him in the face, and now my heart was beating so hard I thought I might puke.

Stephen placed his palm against my chest and I let myself lean back against the wall.

"Are you going to hit me again?" he asked.

I shook my head and then he started to undo my pants. He pulled on the elastic waist of my underwear and took a hold of me. My body shook. Instinct kicked in and I lowered my jeans to the floor. Stephen went to his knees. The blood from his nose and the spit from his mouth glistened against my skin. I closed my eyes, feeling Stephen and thinking of the blood. The sounds he made, the wet sounds, like the slippery sound of zombie carnage lighting up the television screen in my room.

I could hear people screaming for their lives, but I never heard my mother in the hallway, never heard her stifled cry, never heard her slip away from us and back to her room.

Let the gore crescendo until it blows your mind.

I could barely take a breath as I did that very thing.

Stephen cleaned up in the sink. We fell asleep in my room just before dawn.

When I woke up, Stephen was gathering his movies.

"We almost watched them all."

"Pretty close."

"Maybe next time."

And that was how the summer went, watching movies, getting off and reveling in the gore.

The last night Stephen slept over, we watched Dead Alive for the third time. The lights were off, the room barely illuminated by the flickering television. Stephen's face was buried in between my legs and I tugged his hair with my hands, bucking against him. On the television, an undead infant ripped its way through a woman's skull. I smiled, and I turned my head towards the door.

Mother's face in the dark beyond my bedroom, watching.

I froze.

She backed into the pitch and was gone.

Stephen looked up. "What's wrong?"

"Nothing," I said. "Don't stop."

What kind of talk would she want to have in the morning, I wondered? I tried to imagine the horrifying conversations, and then I tried not to imagine anything at all. I wanted a bomb to drop on the house.

I wanted the sun to never rise.

The next morning was uncomfortable and after Stephen left I spent most of it staring at the floor. No one talked. Breakfast was self-serve. To my relief, mother never brought up the incident.

Ever.

Her quiet reservation worried me. She was usually a talker, the kind of person that was happy to offer advice, even if you didn't want it. I used to think that she fancied herself some kind of suburban, feminine Freud. She always had some theory for me and Dad's actions. We never did what we did because it was who we were; we did things because of deep psychological issues that we never confronted.

I can remember the sound of her scrubbing dishes in the sink and yelling things at Dad. "You just like football because your father never told you he loved you," she'd bellow from the kitchen.

"She's crazy," Dad would whisper. Then he'd grab the remote and turn the volume up on the television.

Dad was a guy's guy, you know, a real man's man. He stood a good six feet tall and had broad, strong shoulders. He had thick arms that he would use to swing Momma in circles, mock dancing in the living room. He could pick me up off the ground and toss me in the air. When you're a little kid, that's what God must be like. He enjoyed watching football on television in the winter, and going to baseball games in the summer. Dad could never wrap his mind around the fact that I didn't care for sports. I guess I get it, you know, that he just wanted me to like what he liked. I think he was trying to shape me into the friend that he always wanted.

When summer ended, Stephen went back to mathland. I promised to write, so did he, and for the first week of my junior year of high school I would cry myself to sleep. If I dreamed at all, there were only two things my subconscious would parade through my mind. There was Stephen, and then there were the zombies. Being consumed was either exhilarating or horrifying. Regardless, my sheets were wet when I'd wake up in the morning.

It was after one of the more potent nightmares that I decided to tell my mom that I was in love with Stephen.

As a kid, I hated the sound of footsteps against the wood flooring on the second floor of the house. It usually meant that I was in trouble. My parents rarely bothered to come downstairs for any other reason. It was a custom to walk quietly in the house. Out of sight, out of mind, I suppose.

It was an old place. You could just think about walking around and hear the floors creak and crack. And I was under the belief that my mom could hear a frog fart from a mile radius, so there was no late night runs to the snack cabinet or sneaking out of the house. Hell, I didn't even like going to the bathroom if they were already in bed. Getting in trouble was something to be avoided, and that old house was designed to give me up at the drop of a hat.

I put on a pair of socks and then stepped into the hall.

I was halfway there when I noticed that the door to my mom's room was cracked open, just a little, just enough to let a dim slice of light spill into the hallway. I figured my mother was reading something, maybe one of her paperback romance novels she kept under the bed.

Then I heard my stepdad moan. Mother shushed him over

and over. I don't exactly remember pushing the door, but I remember it opening slowly, like a revelation, and like any revelation, once that door went its course, well, there was no going back.

My stepdad, Eddy, was nude and laid on the bed with his legs hiked up into the air. Mother was on her knees at his waist, blasting him in the ass with a dildo and jerking him off. The look in their eyes disgusted me.

It was passionless.

Empty.

What was it that Stephen said?

Like they're robots. Like they're going through life with their switch turned off. They may as well be asleep.

No, not asleep, I thought.

Dead.

A bit of dialogue ran through my mind. . .

What are they doing? Why do they come here? Some kind of instinct. Memory of what they used to do.

I suddenly forgot why I was there.

My mother froze, not in any kind of abject horror, but more like the way one predator might observe another. It was territorial, for sure. She let go of the dildo, but never the cock.

Eddy's voice broke the pornographic spell, "Jesus Fucking Christ."

And I stumbled backward into the hallway. I heard the shuffling of a bed sheet, the soft whisper of clothes covering flesh.

I ran to my room.

Minutes later, mother knocked on my door.

"Firecracker?" she said.

The door handle jiggled.

"It's locked." I said.

"You just go to bed now. We can talk in the morning."

"Great."

"I'm sorry you had to see that."

"Okay, Mom."

"I guess now you know how it feels."

"Yeah, well now we're even."

Mom ended the conversation by shuffling away from my room and down the hallway, her heels drumming the wooden floors, echoing through the hallways of our dark house. I heard their bedroom door slam. I knew what that meant. I didn't know how she'd say it, but she was going to tell Eddy about Stephen and me. I could feel my stomach drop. The nausea kept me awake through the night.

***

I was afraid of Eddy. Never knew what Mom saw in him. She didn't cry at his funeral like she did at Dad's, though, so maybe Eddy wasn't much more than a warm body to fill the space left by the fire. He was a goddamn nightmare to me.

Eddy poked his head into my room. "You're gonna be late for school if you don't get out of bed."

"Crap." I kicked at my sheets.

"Chop-chop, mister," Eddy clapped his hands. "Your mom's already done left. I gotta get you up or she'll give me the business. Come on, let's go." He clapped again. Eddy was a clapper. He clapped when he wanted something, he clapped when he was mad, and he clapped when Momma made a meal he liked. I even heard him clap in his sleep.

Clap, clap, clap.

"Hey, Eddy," I said. "Sorry about last night."

Eddy stepped into my room. He had his hands on his hips.

Hands on hips, balled into fists.

Shaggy hair hung low over his brow, keeping his eyes in the dark. They were spying on me, as if those twists of brown were curtains and those eyes were seeing something that they weren't supposed to see. He clapped his hands together.

"What I say about the bus now, boy? You got to hurry up and get if I'm gonna take you to school. I got to be on the other side of town, pronto. Let's go. We got some talking to do, too, you and me. Stuff's gonna change around here, you get me? Now hurry up."

Got dressed for school and went upstairs, sat at the kitchen table and tried to prepare myself for whatever was coming. And then I heard the familiar thud of Eddy putting on his shoes, the way he forced his heel down, smacking the floor. I felt every step he took in my chest. The closer he got, the more I began to confuse his steps with my heartbeats. I was welling up before he got to the kitchen door.

"Why are you crying?" he asked.

"I don't know."

"I'm going to ask you one more time." He rolled up his sleeves. "Why are you crying?"

"Because you're going to hit me."

"I'm going to beat your ass right here in this kitchen. I'm going to beat the fucking queer right out of you. And then we're going for a ride to your friend's house. Have a little talk with his folks. See what they have to say about this. Now get up."

My legs lost all feeling. "Please—

He slapped me across the face.

"If you don't get up out of that seat I'm going to lift you up by your damn hair. You hear me?"

. . .that's what God must be like.

My cheek stung and felt impossibly warm, like he hit me hard enough to burn the skin. All I could do was cry. And then he reached out and grabbed me by the hair and lifted me up. He smacked me across the face again.

And again.

All this because of love.

I tried to push him away. He punched me in the stomach and I dropped to the floor.

"I'll be waiting in the car. And you do not want to *keep* me waiting, you understand? Because I'll come looking for you, and . . ."

Eddy's lips were moving, but his words trailed off.

Sound had disappeared.

Eddy didn't know what was coming. But I did. And I smiled.

Every moment slowed down. I could see between the seconds.

Time ceased.

Eddy's eyes rolled up. His mouth drooped. He stumbled, fell into a heap on the floor.

The curtain of reality rippled and pulled apart. Eyes like dying stars. Shadow and fog.

Death looked at me from the void outside of time and spoke with a voice that was like a shimmer of light in the furthest reaches of memory, like a song you struggle to remember or a name you once knew.

"Do you want to know when I will come for you?"

"Yes," I said without hesitation.

Death whispered in my mind and I've been waiting ever since.

***

A crossed path is its own intimacy.

***

When Death found me at the back of The Night Cap, it was as though the whole world went under and swam in the cold black and we were alone upon an island, hearing and seeing nothing because then there was nothing else, except love—that single star revolving—which focused all its light and heat unto me and I knew it was time to burn alive.

You are one of them, one of us, an infinite being

The dream never ends

None of this is real

And it wasn't just my life passing before my eyes, but the lives of those I loved, and I could no longer tell where my dream ended and their dreams began. The reward for a life lived. No more secrets. No more ghosts.

I left myself and left reality and I could finally see time for what it was.

An infinite circle.

***

Time I am, the great destroyer of the worlds.

74

***

Every mother and father is a little ship that escorts its passenger from oblivion to a world of flesh and blood. We are all immigrants, from a land that can only be compared to a sleep without dreams. We assimilate by learning the culture and struggling with the language, the customs. And these are usually imparted to us by our captains, in the hope that we can someday become captains ourselves, and be ready to teach whatever passengers may come aboard our own little ship sailing in the sea of finite time.

***

What about the flies?

What about what?

The flies . . . did you ask them?

She hadn't. She didn't consider the idea. Ask the flies . . . what was that supposed to mean?

Flies have been around for a long time. If anyone will know, it will be them.

They're just flies.

That's true. They are just flies. You are just a little girl. What do you know, little girl? Do you know where your mother and father are?

No, no I don't.

Would you like to find out?

She nodded.

Then let's ask the flies.

The flies scattered when she tried to approach. She looked to Death.

You don't have to chase them, just ask.

She didn't take a step, but turned and glared at the flies. They began to regroup.

There's so many of them. Which one do I ask?

Just ask. If one knows, then they all will.

She watched. A group of ten flies became twenty, then one hundred, and then a great buzzing hum. She looked above at the swirling mass, the living cloud of black bugs and their beating wings.

She asked her question.

"Love," buzzed the flies in response.

She cried.

***

I watched an obese boy in a red shirt. He reminded me of a candy apple. I wonder what kind of treat I remind people of. I can only hope they are more kind than I am.

His mother's dog, barking, inside their house, sees nothing.

I wonder what will happen to the dog. Sometime later, I find out it was put to sleep.

Emily moved closer to me, never taking her eyes off mine. She breathed through her mouth. I feel her breath blanket my neck and run smoothly across my chin.

Why can't you touch me?

I'm afraid.

You watch me during class. I've caught you but you always look away. She closes her eyes and leans toward me. What are you afraid of?

Nothing.

Her skin tells me that I am not alone. Our kiss is nothing less than the death of stars at the beginning of time, a warm truth, illuminating everything.

***

The smell of my own burning hair creeps through the kaleidoscope and brings me back to The Night Cap, for a moment, and I catch a couple bars of a song I heard, years ago, and that I played obsessively for Emily after we were married.

It's funny how some albums, some songs, are like a séance that conjures up ghosts, the ghosts of moments, the look on someone's face years ago, the uncertainty before first embraces, holding hands, being alone, being a ghost in any given moment, really.

We are all machines meant to record, that consume recordings through our ears and our eyes and everything is playing on a constant loop, so as to create facsimiles of recorded moments, simultaneously recording them and experiencing them, again and again.

I miss different people on different days and I try to get out the old recordings to play them, but they are wearing out.

At some point, you lose it all and what you are left with is knowing that you lived, that you heard a voice, saw a face, touched another human being.

We yearn for one another until we can only yearn for the facsimile, then at the end we have neither and we are forced—ourselves—to become a recording, a ghost, to be remembered during someone else's séance, someone else's favorite song.

My eardrums burst. All my hair is gone. The kaleidoscope returns.

All the dead—once children—dreaming and unable to wake
. . . for dream is now reality, unknowable and infinite.

***

A MAN WITH THE FIRE INSIDE HIM

That was the headline. Or, at least, that's what I remember it saying.

It came with a certain amount of notoriety. News folks covered it when it happened and news folks still ask about it from time to time. Everybody wants to hear about the Act of God, about the spontaneous combustion. I was even on the tube a couple of times, once on a local show and another time was for some fancy cable show all about goofy stuff like UFOs and the Loch Ness Monster and God knows what, I don't know.

I never had cable.

Now that you know about my daddy and all, well, I guess I ought to get into real quick as to why I was thinking about it at all, why you should know about it. Why you should know about me, in a roundabout kind of way, because Momma seemed to think I got a lot of what made Daddy, well, Daddy, I guess.

"Firecracker is just the spitting image of his poppa, don't you think?"

It was a question I'd heard her ask over and over 'til she finally died, and even after she was gone I could still hear her asking.

The thing is, I never really knew how much I actually am like my daddy, or like my daddy was, rather. I didn't know until I got a little older, a little longer in the tooth. If I had to compare it to something, getting older, I mean, I guess I'd have to say that it's a lot like opening a window, because damned if the years just don't show you a bunch of things you never saw before. The thing about it is—getting older—the thing that window showed me more clear than anything else, was me. And I don't mean like no damn mirror, because that's just the surface, just a reflection, and I don't need any clarification on that. I got a mirror in my bathroom. I know what I look like. No, I mean a window that looks out over a great yard that's just packed with everything you ever did, and everything you know your mom and pop ever did and on and on. I look out that window long enough, and I can finally see Firecracker.

In a funny way, seeing me was a lot like seeing my daddy. Some call it sins of the father, I guess, but scientifically I think we can all agree we are just bits and pieces of our parents anyhow. So, I got to thinking about Daddy, about how he burst into flames when I was a kid, about how he could appreciate a good looking woman and how he and I would watch Mackeninny sunbathe in the summer.

Sometimes, when I'm missing Dad, I'll cruise on by the Wood River pool. Daddy loved that pool. I love it now.

Like I said, I'm a lot like my dad.

And I got the fire inside me.

***

Everybody is dead.

None of this is real. The dream never ends.

You are one of them, one of us, an infinite being.

***

"You've been spying on me for years," I say.

"I've been watching you fall in love," Death says.

"I wasn't *falling* in love, I was *in* love. With her. Always."

"Love is nothing but trouble. And pain."

"Maybe that's the way it is for you." I say. "Because you are always on the other side of the curtain, looking in, you can only see the pain. But you don't see what's inside. Not while we are alive."

"I won't let you remember her name. Why should I?"

"You could tell me."

"No, it's not good enough," Death says. "I had to change the way you see her. I had to reinterpret her, so you could see her for what she really is."

"You're speaking in riddles," I say.

"We can have something and at the same time know what it is to have nothing at all. Love is the confirmation of that, because when we love someone we love their presence and their absence."

"Love is better than that."

"Love is no more than another commodity. It tricks you into believing you have everything, but in the end it leaves you with nothing. It is loneliness incarnate. I couldn't let you fall into that trap."

"You can't make those kinds of decisions for people."

"By giving you pain I'm saving you from it."

"Maybe love is a pain that I want to have," I say. "Maybe that is what we are all really searching for. Loneliness. Maybe you need to feel that pain to know you were ever happy at all."

"You really think that?"

"I don't think anything. I don't have answers. All I can do is tell you how I feel."

"And you would rather feel love's inevitable pain, than be free of it?"

"Yes."

"Do you read much poetry, Firecracker?"

"No."

"Did you know that poetry has to be read in order for it to survive?"

"Enough riddles, Death."

"No. This isn't a riddle. If someone writes a poem and no one reads it, then that poem dies. You have to give yourself to the poem in order for it to live. You have to experience it to make life."

"Poetry won't bring her back to me."

"Of course it will."

"Are you being serious?"

"People have to experience other people to really live, and there is no experience so intimate as giving life, whether it is to flesh or to words. After you danced together, there was poetry. Search your mind and she will live in those words."

"Thank you," I say.

"I want to help you as much as I have to hurt you," Death

says.

"I love you, too."

***

I can no longer remember her name.

But we met when I was fifteen. We were both freshmen in high school. We got to know each other at a theater camp that year. She was an only child. Lived with her aunt.

Her mother had killed her dad one night over dinner, about a year earlier.

She was still going to therapy over it. Not that she was crazy or anything, but she was traumatized. She would talk about it like it happened to someone else. She would tell me about dreams where she talked to flies and how she thought the flies were her parents trying to speak to her from another reality. It may have sounded crazy to someone else, but I don't know, I guess it wasn't too different from how I'd talk about Dad.

She said she started writing poetry to help get over her emotions. It was a suggestion by her therapist, I think. She gave me two of her poems, Regretful and lonely getaway, during that year's last week of school. She moved away and I haven't seen her since. The last I heard, she was living on the West Coast. Married, I think, to someone very lucky.

I ask to see her hand, look at her thumb. I see our hands side by side,
wondering:
about touching her hand tasting her palm with nails she laughs
snaking through her fingers hold her face as if I'm in Klimt's Kiss
feel smooth features with my eyes pull her curved parts to mine
my hand runs up the back of her head as if coming up for air we kiss
"Your thumb is so small," I smile, and look into her pillow-eyes:
Daydreaming

I drift

from reality on a boat

somewhere in my eyes.

I look

At patterns in tile

and shapes in the ceiling.

I notice

a large boy

in a bright red cotton shirt.

I wonder

what kind of fruit

people see me as?

I hope

that they have better taste

than myself

I hate

taking these trips

alone.

***

I can no longer remember her name.

But I remember that we had an art class with another student, Alex. She had always been infatuated with Alex, and of course she told me all about it. Alex was a pretty cool kid but we were young and she wasn't ready for that kind of relationship. A lot of people weren't ready for that, I guess.

We wanted to be ready, but we were fooling ourselves.

She wrote a poem about Alex. I don't really know what to say about it. She told me that she didn't want to use any punctuation in her thoughts. She believed that her thoughts were better expressed in a continuous stream.

She mentions an artist in the poem, Klimt. He was a painter. He did a lot of romantic, erotic pieces. That's how she saw things, with a sense of artistic passion.

Lonely getaway was written during a history class or math class. I doubt that it is really of any importance to the poem. She was bored. It was, after all, just another high school class. She would space out if a teacher lost her interest. She really would stare at the ceiling sometimes. It was funny to me. She talked about daydreaming as if it were some kind of boat ride, like a vacation.

I think lonely getaway is her way of coming to grips with her parents. She used to tell me that, no matter what she thought of, it always came back to them. She felt abandoned by them. She was, really. Her mom is still in jail and they scattered her dad's ashes. She lived with her mom's sister until she turned eighteen.

She would tell me that she visited them, her parents, in her daydreams. It was the only place that they existed for her anymore. Her dad had no grave for her to visit and I'm not sure she ever spoke with her mom again. She told me that her parents had become nothing more than the sum of memories. Memories, she told me, had become something like a seaside town where she could go see her mom and dad.

I think that she tortured herself about her parents. I am pretty sure that the poetry was reinforcing how hurt and insecure she was. She wrote this in my senior yearbook:

"I think we ought to read only the kinds of books that wound and stab us. . .we need the books that affect us like a disaster, that grieve us deeply, like the death of someone we loved more than ourselves, like being banished into forests far from everyone, like a suicide. A book must be the axe for the frozen sea inside us." –Kafka-

And that was how we parted.

I think about her a lot. She's the only person that ever made me laugh, truly and deeply. I wrote a poem for her that I ended up throwing in the garbage. Not giving that poem to her is one of my biggest regrets. I remember every line.

A body begs to be seen
for its curves to be fondled by the eyes

the air between us like velvet pressing water

no harm comes from a glance

And no matter how many times I see, it will always be the first
it will always be the most fantastic

a radiant, uncompromising grip on my attention
to miss this chance is like missing out on air
or gravity?

Presence creates an undeniable pressure
In my voyeur mind, lost in vineyards of attraction

Could it be that I'm forgetting to breathe
Or is it the pull of an intense physical attraction

If I could only be allowed in this atmosphere
that I may graze the surface
without burning on entry

Her name, I realize, isn't important. That I loved her is all that matters and I let the memory of her go. And it occurs to me that if time is a circle and I am forever, then this poem wasn't written only for her.

I wrote it for all of them.

***

"Would you hold my hand?" Emily asks.

I nod. "Yes."

"What are you thinking?"

"I don't know." I look at her. We are deadlocked. "I think I like you."

"I like you, too, Martin." She winds her fingers through mine and I am on the brink of having a cold sweat. I feel a rush of cool in my arms and chest.

The moment she said my name I knew I loved her.

I am stuck in an elevator with a boy named Stephen and his dead mother, I am stuck in there with my mother and father, but all I can see now is Emily. I put my arms around the girl, and she does the same to me. I can feel her fingers on my back and for the first time I feel like I am greeting someone instead of saying goodbye. Cold chills change to a blanket of warmth that envelops us, bathes us in a red, candy-apple glow.

***

The seconds slow to a crawl and I know that Death is watching but I do not look at him.

Instead . . .

I think about love.

***

And I burst into flames.

95

***

And I burst into flames.

AFTERWORD

I started writing AT THE END OF THE DAY I BURST INTO FLAMES many, many years ago. At least, I think, as far back as 1999. Originally, the book was titled THE INFINITE ZOMBIE HYPOTHESIS, being informed more by innocence than experience, and the narrative was quite a bit different than what it ultimately became. And for the better! Truly, back then, I was writing for an audience of one. Getting published wasn't something I actively considered, and amusing myself was the order of the day. But there were bits of the prose that sang to me, stuck with me well after I'd written them, and every few years I'd revisit what I had scribbled, adding to it or stealing good bits for other manuscripts.

That seems to be the way I work, though. An idea creeps in, and I set my mind to fleshing out outlandish concepts, letting narratives get as messy as possible before I do one of two things: exhaust myself and abandon the concept; see a narrative through to the bitter end. After small, surprising success with NECROSAURUS REX in 2014, I found myself faced with the task of creating a follow-up book. Luckily, for me, I had been working on that follow-up for the last fifteen years.

Only once have I checked myself into a hotel in order to finish a manuscript and AT THE END OF THE DAY I BURST INTO FLAMES holds that distinction. I like to think it wasn't far removed from what it must have been like, sitting in a smoky room in Tangiers, piecing together the scattered, mad thoughts that would become NAKED LUNCH. The difference being that I had no help, no pack of talented authors to wrangle sobriety from my ramblings, and the indisputable fact that Klamath Falls is no Tangiers. What I *had* was a hidden narrative before me, and I gave myself 48 hours to dig it out.

I did not sleep that weekend, but I did finish my book. Ultimately, what helped me crack through the mess and fashion a narrative was that old chestnut: *kill your darlings*. No more "*infinite zombie hypothesis*" and all that entailed. I killed so many darlings over the course of two days. Much of the genre-heavy elements were cut completely in favor of a brutally honest, confessional style. By taking what I had and making it *less*, I made it *more*.

AT THE END OF THE DAY I BURST INTO FLAMES is worthy of rediscovery, I think. The slim book is a personal favorite of my own works, and remains some of my very best writing. What it lacked, unfortunately, was an audience. Here's hoping that this reprint helps the book burn a little brighter than before…

ABOUT THE AUTHOR

Nicholas Day is the author of GRIND YOUR BONES TO DUST, NECROSAURUS REX, and OCTOBER ANIMALS. His short fiction is frequently anthologized. He co-owns Rooster Republic Press with Don Noble, where they acquire and produce award-winning horror fiction and poetry.

Currently, he resides in Northern Illinois with his family, and he is always working on new material. You can find more information about him and his work at nicholasdayonline.com